Here are some other
Redfeather Chapter Books
you will enjoy:

Hot Fudge Hero
by Pat Brisson
illustrated by Diana Cain Bluthenthal

Little Sister, Big Sister
by Pat Brisson
illustrated by Diana Cain Bluthenthal

Marty Frye, Private Eye
by Janet Tashjian
illustrated by Laurie Keller

The Friendship of
Milly *and* Tug

The Friendship of
Milly *and* Tug

by Dian Curtis Regan
illustrated by Jennifer Danza

A Redfeather Chapter Book
Henry Holt and Company
New York

Henry Holt and Company, Inc., *Publishers since 1866*
115 West 18th Street, New York, New York 10011

Henry Holt is a registered trademark of Henry Holt and Company, Inc.

Library of Congress Cataloging-in-Publication Data
Regan, Dian Curtis.
The friendship of Milly and Tug / by Dian Curtis Regan; illustrated by Jennifer Danza.
    p.   cm.—(A redfeather chapter book)
Summary: Milly the cat and her friend Tug the mouse challenge each other to a
spelling contest, argue about who is a better actor, and have other adventures.
    [1. Friendship—Fiction.   2. Cats—Fiction.   3. Mice—Fiction.]
    I. Danza, Jennifer, ill.   II. Title.   III. Series.
    PZ7.R25854Fr   1999   [Fic]—dc21   98-38100

ISBN 0-8050-5935-0 / First Edition—1999
Printed in Mexico
1 3 5 7 9 10 8 6 4 2

For Alexis Canfield and Patterson Jaffurs

–D. C. R.

For my mom and dad, who sacrificed everything

–J. D.

Contents

The Friendship of
Milly ^{and} Tug

The Spelling Bee

"What are you doing?" asked Milly the cat,
early one summer morning.

"I am making a list of words I can spell,"
answered Tug the mouse.

Milly peered over Tug's head.

"How do you know they are spelled right?"

"Because I am a master speller," Tug said.

"Prove it," Milly snipped.

"I can spell a word that has six letters."

Tug wrote in the dirt so Milly could see:

Flower

"So what?" Milly told him. "I can spell
a word with seven letters."

"Prove it," Tug snipped back.

Milly wrote next to Tug's word:

Flowers

"You copied!" Tug yelped.

"I did not!" Milly snarled.

"Then we will have a spelling bee to see who knows the most words."

"I'll keep score," Milly said.

"What is my first word?"

Hmmm, Tug thought. "Spell *rock*."

"That's easy," Milly scoffed. "R-O-C."

"No! That's not right.

It needs one more letter," Tug said.

"OK," Milly groaned.

"You are right," Tug sighed.

"It needed a *k*. R-O-C-K."

Pleased, Milly wrote in the dirt with a stick:

Milly 1 tug 0

"What is *my* first word?" Tug asked.

Milly scratched her ear. "Spell *chickadee*."

"What?" Tug cried. "That's a hard word."

"But you are a master speller," reminded Milly.

Tug walked in circles.

He knew a chickadee was a bird,

but he did not know how to spell

such a long word.

Suddenly it came to him.

"I've got it!" Tug yelped. "B-I-R-D."

Milly did not know if the word

was right or wrong because

she was not a master speller. "I thought

chickadee had more letters than that."

"Some of them are silent," Tug explained.

"Oh," said Milly. She changed the score:

Milly 1   tug 1

Tug looked up and down and all
around for a good word. "*Cloud*," he said.

Milly closed her eyes to think. "K—"

"Wrong!" blurted Tug.

"I was not finished," Milly grumped.

"Go on, then," Tug insisted. "Spell it."

"I-T," spelled Milly.

"What?" Tug was confused.

7

"You said spell *it*, so I spelled it. I-T,"
Milly giggled.

Tug did not like being tricked.

"Here is your next word," Milly said.
"*Petunia*."

Tug frowned. "That's too hard."

"Not for a master speller," argued Milly.

Tug pointed at the first word in the dirt:

Flower

Puzzled, Milly stared at the word.

"Are some of the letters silent?"

"Yes," Tug said. "Most of them."

"Wow," exclaimed Milly.

"W-O-W," spelled Tug.

"I was *not* giving you a word
to spell," Milly snapped.

Tug changed the score anyway:

Milly 2   tug 3

"Now it's my turn to give you a word," he said.
Grinning, Tug rubbed his paws together.
Milly looked worried. "Maybe we should
play another game," she said.
"It's hard to win a spelling bee
against a master speller."

She circled Tug's name and wrote:
Winur in the dirt.

Tug liked being the winner even if
Milly spelled it wrong. He would let his friend
catch up by giving her an easy word.
"Spell *bee*," Tug told her.
Milly wrote in the dirt:
Be

Tug almost hollered "Wrong!"
but caught himself.
The word was *not* wrong.
He and Milly both were right.
"Sometimes there is more
than one way to spell a word," Tug said.
"That is the first rule
a master speller must learn."
Next to Milly's name, Tug wrote:
Winner #2

Milly's Play

In the afternoon,

Tug could not find Milly.

She was not sunning herself

in the kitchen window.

She was not napping beneath the bed.

She was not cleaning her whiskers

in the cool shade on the back step.

Tug raced into the woods behind the house.

"Milly!" he called. "Where are you?"

Strange noises led him to a

big rock with bushes all around.

He found Milly posed on top of the rock.

"What are you doing?" asked Tug.

"Ummff," said Milly. "I am acting.

I want to be onstage like my aunt."

Milly struck another pose.

"Angora was more famous

in all nine of her lives

than most cats are in one."

"Angora?" repeated Tug.

"Ummff!" cried Milly.

"You have never heard of her?"

"Was she ever in a mouse play?" Tug asked.

"Of course not! Why would a famous
cat actress be in a mouse play? Ummff!"
"Why do you keep saying
'Ummff'?" Tug asked.
"Because it was Angora's favorite word.
She ummffed through every play.
Her fans loved it."

Tug was excited about acting
and saying "Ummff! Ummff! Ummff!"
"May I be in your play?" he asked.
"Cats are fabulous actors," Milly told him.
"But a mouse cannot act."
"I can yodel," Tug offered.
"I do not have a part for a yodeler,"
Milly scoffed.

"I can sing the alphabet song."

Tug cleared his throat and began,

"A, B, C, D—"

"I know the song," Milly grumped.

"But there is no music in my play.

It's a drama.

Angora was best at weeping," she said.

Milly hunched her back and began to weep.

"Milly!" Tug cried. "What's wrong?"

Milly licked a paw, looking pleased.

"Nothing is wrong. I was acting."

"Oh, please let me be in your play," Tug begged.

He knew he could not weep as well as Milly,

but he could try.

"A mouse cannot act," Milly insisted,

"but maybe you can be the crew.

A play needs a crew."

"What does a crew do?" asked Tug.

"Move that branch," Milly ordered.

Tug moved the branch.

The sun shone brightly on Milly's face.

"You turned the spotlight on me,"
she said. "That is what a crew does."

"But I want to act," Tug whimpered.

"I bet I can do it if you just let me try."

Milly pranced across her rock stage.

"A mouse cannot act!" she proclaimed loudly,
almost as if she were acting.

 Tug rolled his eyes.

"You have said that three times."

"Then it must be true," Milly told him.

Tug climbed to the highest tip of the rock.

"If you will not let me act," he warned,

"I will go home and play by myself."

Suddenly his paw slipped.

He toppled off the rock

and rolled over

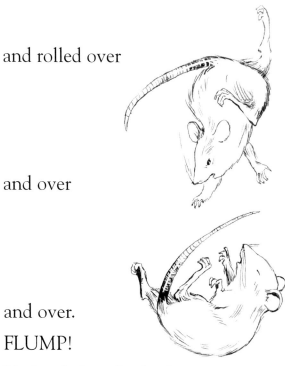

and over

and over.
FLUMP!
He landed in the bushes
at the foot of Milly's stage.

"Tug!" Milly yowled. She leaped to
her friend's side. "Are you hurt?"
Milly licked Tug's face. "Please be all right.
I am sorry I would not let you act in my play."
Tug sprang to his feet.

"Oh, my!" Milly cried. "I thought
you were dead!"
"I was not dead," Tug gloated. "I was acting!"
He bowed with great style.

"I also had a famous aunt—
daring Aunt Rhodant.
She fell off many stages in her day.
I want to be just like her," Tug said.
Milly scampered back onto the stage.

"Well, I guess my play has a part
for a mouse actor after all," she said.
"Ummff!" Tug cried.
"I am not a mouse actor."
He grabbed a tree branch
and swung to the top of the stage.
"I am a stunt mouse!"

Good Fortune

A noise woke Milly
from her afternoon nap.
It was Tug.
He marched past in hiking clothes,
with a knapsack on his back.
"Where are you going?" asked Milly.
"I'm off to seek good fortune," Tug replied.
Milly yawned and stretched. "Why?" she said.
"Because that is what heroes in storybooks do."
Tug marched down the road.

"Wait!" called Milly.

"How do you know good fortune is that way?"

Tug looked up and down the road.

"What if good fortune

is the other way?" Milly insisted.

Tug did not know the answer.

"I will find it," he told her,

hoping he sounded brave like a hero.

Tug started off again.

Milly padded after him.

"What is it this time?" Tug asked.

"Will you be home for supper?" she said.

Milly shared her supper crunchies with Tug.

Tug loved Milly's supper crunchies.

"I will try," he promised. "Now, good-bye."

Tug hurried down the road and around a bend.

He had never been this far

from Milly's house.

The bushes seemed fatter.

Noises seemed louder.

Shadows melted when he turned to look.

Tug stopped to wave at Milly,

but she was out of sight.

He began to yodel softly

to keep from feeling scared.

Ahead lay a meadow.

"Maybe good fortune is waiting for me
in that meadow," Tug exclaimed.
He raced into the tall grass
but couldn't see over it.
Then he spotted a rock.

"Maybe I can view the meadow
from up there," Tug said.
He scampered to the tip-top
and peered all around.
"If good fortune is here,
I do not see it."
Tug began to wonder what good fortune
looked like.

He hopped to the ground and started off again.
Soon tall grass gave way to trees.
Perhaps good fortune waited in the forest—
even though it looked dark and spooky.

Tug took a deep breath and started off into
the woods.

Flap! Flap! Flap!

He dove for a hole in a tree stump.

A hawk swooshed overhead.

Tug shivered. "This is not good fortune!"

He hid until the hawk was out of sight.

Tug dashed through the forest

until he was in the sunshine again.

A sparkly lake lay before him.

He sat on the shore to catch his breath

and eat the snack from his knapsack.

Good fortune was not in the meadow.

Good fortune was not in the woods.

"Maybe good fortune is on the lake," Tug said.

"I will build a boat and sail away,

like a hero in a storybook."

But no one was around
to help him build a boat.
He missed Milly.
He missed their cozy napping spots.
He missed sharing snacks.

Tug found a sturdy piece of bark
and a twig to hoist a leaf.
It made a perfect sail.
Tug pushed his boat into the water
and sailed away.

In the middle of the lake,

the wind began to blow.

WHOOOOOOOSH!

The boat tipped!

The sail ripped!

Splash!

Tug held tight to his knapsack

and watched his boat sink.

"Help!" he cried in a tiny voice

because he was too scared to shout.

35

The waves knocked Tug about.

He tried to yodel

but water filled his mouth.

He tried to purr like Milly

because her purring always calmed him.

But a mouse cannot purr.

SPLOOOOOOOSH!

Tug shut his eyes tight.

He felt water rushing past.

Then he felt sand beneath his paws.

Was he safe?

Tug slowly opened his eyes

and tried to catch his breath.

He did not feel like a hero.

He would never find good fortune.

And now he wanted to hear Milly's purr

more than anything in the world.

Tug wrung out his shirt

and lifted his wet knapsack.

He started down the road,

but he did not know where he was,

or where he was going.

Soon he came to a sunny spot.

It looked just right for napping,

so Tug curled up and went to sleep.

He dreamed Milly's house was nearby.

He dreamed Milly was napping beside him.

He could almost hear her purring.

Then he heard an even more wonderful sound:

Supper crunchies falling into a bowl!

Tug woke up and leaped to his feet.

"You came home for supper," Milly exclaimed.

"Just like you promised."

Tug did not know how he got home,

but he was happy to be here.

"Did you find good fortune?" Milly asked.

Tug looked at his yummy supper.

He looked at the cozy napping spot.

And he looked at his best friend

who shared it all with him.

"Yes," he said. "I found good fortune."

"Then you are a hero," Milly told him.

"Just like in a storybook."

"I knew that," Tug boasted.

He puffed his chest and felt quite brave—

a hero in his own backyard.

Tug's Bedtime Tale

That night,

the air was hot and the moon was full.

Milly and Tug could not sleep.

They lay down in the tall cool grass

at the edge of the forest.

"Tell me a bedtime tale," Tug whispered,

"so I will fall asleep."

Milly curled into a ball and gazed at the stars.

"I will tell you a story about a cat

named Dagger."

"Dagger?" Tug's eyes flew open.

"That was his name," Milly explained,

"because his teeth were sharp

and pointy like knives."

Tug shivered.

"Dagger prowls on nights

when the moon is full," Milly added.

"Like tonight?" Tug asked in a whisper.

Milly stared at the full moon. "Like tonight."

Tug sat up and perked his ears.

"Most cats hunt for dinner," Milly went on,

"but Dagger hunts for fun."

"For fun?" Tug echoed.

"Yes. Hunting is a sport to Dagger

because he is quick and quiet."

Tug raised to his tiptoes to peer

over the tall grass.

"How quick and quiet is he?"

"So quick and quiet," Milly said,

"you never know he is coming."

Tug's gaze darted back and forth.

His teeth began to chatter.

"Do you know D-Dagger?" he asked.

"Oh, yes," Milly exclaimed. "He is my cousin.

He has promised to visit.
Since you are my best friend
in the whole world,
you will get to meet him."

Tug's legs began to wobble.
"W-When do you think he will visit?"
"Soon," Milly said.
Tug's heart raced in circles.
He teetered on his tiptoes,
swaying to the left,
swaying to the right.

Then he fainted.

KERRRRRRPLOP!

"Oh, good!" Milly cried.

"My bedtime tale did the trick.

It made dear Tug go to sleep."

Milly's story had made her sleepy too.

She snuggled close to her very best friend

and soon fell fast asleep.

A True Story

In the morning, Tug was a happy mouse.

Dagger, the cat, had not come to visit.

He felt safe, reading with Milly

in the shade of a leafy apple tree—

even though his book was scary.

"This is a spooky story!" Tug exclaimed.

"It makes me shiver."

"My book is sad," Milly told him.

"It makes me cry."

She sniffed to prove her point.

"I would like to write a book," Milly added.

"A happy story that makes me smile."

"Me too," Tug agreed.

Milly closed her book. "I've got a great idea.
Let's write a book together!"

"What about?" asked Tug.

"About us," Milly declared.

"Good idea," Tug said.

"It is rare for a mouse to be a cat's best friend."

"Right," Milly agreed.

"A mouse is usually a cat's best dinner."

She found a good writing stick

and gave it to Tug because

he was a master speller.

"Let's call our book

MILLY AND TUG," said Milly.

Tug was quiet.

"What is wrong?" she asked.

"I do not like your title," Tug told her.

"Our book should be called

TUG AND MILLY."

"Why?" Milly asked.

"Because it sounds better," answered Tug.

"Writing a book together was *my* idea,

so *my* name comes first."

Tug wrote:

Milly and tug

even though he did not like it.

"Read what we have written so far,"
ordered Milly.

"So far," Tug told her,

"all we have written is our title.

What comes next?" he asked.

"Next comes a dedication," Milly explained.

"A dedication to someone special."

Milly and Tug were quiet while
they wrote their dedications.

"Read yours first," said Milly.

"This book," Tug read, "is for my mother."

Milly wrinkled her nose. "This is *our* book.
It cannot be dedicated to *your* mother.
Your mother is a mouse!" she snarled.
"Well, *of course* my mother is a mouse,"
Tug snipped. "Read your dedication."
"This book," Milly read, "is for *my* mother."

Tug gasped. "Our book cannot be dedicated
to *your* mother. Your mother is a cat!"
Tug was so upset,
he scampered up and down a hollyhock stalk.
"No mouse in his right mind would read a
book dedicated to a cat!"
Milly hissed. "You have insulted my mother."

"Well, you insulted my mother first,"
Tug grumped.
Milly and Tug turned their backs
on each other.

Soon Milly said, "I have a new dedication."
She scribbled in the dirt:
this book is for our mothers
"That," Tug agreed, "is a perfect dedication."
"Now," said Milly. "How should
our book begin?"
"Like all good books." Tug wrote:
Once upon a time

"I like it," said Milly. "What comes next?"

"The story."

"What story?"

"The story we have to make up," Tug told her.

"Oh," Milly sighed. "This is not going to be easy."

Milly and Tug thought for a long, long time.

"Read what we have so far," Milly asked.

"Once upon a time…," Tug began.

Milly waited. "Is that all?"

"That's all," Tug said.

Milly groaned. "Wow. Writing a book
is hard work."
She yawned and stretched. "It makes
me sleepy."

Tug yawned, too. "Let's take a nap.
Maybe our story will come to us in a dream."
In no time at all, Milly was cat-snoring.

Soon Tug was mouse-dreaming.

"Eeek!" Tug eeeked.

Milly leaped to her feet and puffed her tail.

"What is wrong?" she cried.

Tug's heart thump-thumped.

"I dreamed I was snitching cheese
in the kitchen when a broom came down
on top of me."

"Oh, no!" cried Milly.

"That cannot be our story.

It is a scary story that makes me shiver."

"What did you dream?" asked Tug.

"I dreamed I was cold and hungry and lost.

Then you eeeked and woke me up."

"That is a sad story," groaned Tug.

"It makes me cry."

"That's it!" Milly yelped.

"We dreamed our own true story.

That is how we became best friends."

Tug remembered…

"The broom swept me out the back door,
but I held on to the cheese."

"And when you tumbled off the porch,"
Milly added, "you found me hiding
beneath the step."

"You were a lost kitten," Tug told her.

"Without a home."

"You gave me the cheese to eat," Milly said.

"Well, I had to," Tug answered coyly.

"You were crying."

Milly sniffled at the memory.

"You told me to stay by the back door
and I would be fed," she added.

"And I was right," Tug reminded her.

Milly wiped a tear from her whiskers.

"Then I promised I would never hurt you."

"You saved my life, dear Tug."

"Gosh," Tug said as he scratched their story in the dirt with a stick.

"You were just a baby."

Milly licked Tug's face.

"And we have been best friends ever since."

Tug made sure his letters were neat.

"Look, Milly. Our book is finished. And it is a happy story that makes us smile."

Milly took the stick from Tug's paw.

"It needs one more thing."

Then she wrote the perfect ending:

Milly and tug lived
happily ever after!
the end